Big Anthony

HIS STORY

Tomie dePaola

PUFFIN BOOKS

For Mother Phyllis; Chairman Mgt;
Doug, "the guy in the suit;" and
my arty, foodie friend, Cecilia

PUFFIN BOOKS
Published by the Penguin Group
Penguin Putnam Books for Young Readers, 345 Hudson Street, New York, New York 10014, U.S.A.
Penguin Books Ltd, 27 Wrights Lane, London W8 5TZ, England
Penguin Books Australia Ltd, Ringwood, Victoria, Australia
Penguin Books Canada Ltd, 10 Alcorn Avenue, Toronto, Ontario, Canada M4V 3B2
Penguin Books (N.Z.) Ltd, 182-190 Wairau Road, Auckland 10, New Zealand

Penguin Books Ltd, Registered Offices: Harmondsworth, Middlesex, England

First published in the United States of America by G. P. Putnam's Sons, a member of The Putnam & Grosset Group, 1998
Published by Puffin Books, a division of Penguin Putnam Books for Young Readers, 2001

7 9 10 8

Copyright © Tomie dePaola, 1998
All rights reserved

THE LIBRARY OF CONGRESS HAS CATALOGED THE G. P. PUTNAM'S SONS EDITION AS FOLLOWS:
dePaola, Tomie. Big Anthony: his story. p. cm.
Summary: Big Anthony, well-meaning but inattentive, journeys around Italy
causing one problem after another, before meeting Strega Nona.
[1. Attention—Fiction. 2. Italy—Fiction.]
I. Title. PZ7.D439Bf 1998 [E]—dc21 97-40084 CIP AC
ISBN 0-399-23189-7

This edition ISBN 978-0-698-11893-5

Printed in the United States of America

It was a beautiful sunny day on a farm in the northern hills of the country we now know as Italy.

Everything was set for a big feast.

The whole family was gathered at the door of the farmhouse.

"Here comes the *bambino*," Zia Rosetta, the aunt, called out. The godparents, carrying a fine baby boy, walked out, followed by a beaming mama and a proud papa.

"On to the church," *il padrino*—the godfather—announced. "This will be the happiest of days. This is the firstborn, and he will do great things."

"After all," said Nonno Emilio, the grandfather, "children are our future."

Everyone crowded into the church for the christening. The godparents held the baby as everyone gathered around. The baby was fast asleep. Mama whispered softly, "Wake up, my son, and listen to *Padre* Marcello."

The priest started to pour the holy water as he declared, "Henceforth you shall be known as Anthony."

Just then baby Anthony, who was still asleep, threw up his arm,
spilling the holy water all over himself and everyone else.

"Look. Baby Anthony didn't even cry or wake up when he got all
wet," Zia Rosetta whispered to Nonna Graziella, his grandmother.
"What a good *bambino*."

"Hmmm," Nonna Graziella said as she watched everyone drying off.
"I don't know..."

On little Anthony's first birthday there was a feast of all feasts. In the shade of the olive grove, the family and friends sat at tables piled high with food. On a separate table was the birthday cake. Papa stood to give a birthday greeting.

"Sit quietly, my son, and listen to Papa," Mama whispered to little Anthony. Papa began to make a speech. It was a long speech. "And now," Papa said, "*Felice Compleanno*—Happy Birthday—to my little son." But little Anthony was nowhere to be seen.

Suddenly there was a loud crash. Everyone looked around, and there was little Anthony, covered in cake.

"Hmmm," Nonna Graziella said. "Little Anthony may be a bit of trouble."

Little Anthony began to grow.

"He's going to be a big boy," Nonno Emilio said. "He takes after my side of the family."

Soon it was time for little Anthony to learn to drink out of a cup.
Nonna Graziella was going to teach him.
"Hold your cup in both hands." Anthony did.

"Lift it up." And Anthony did.   "Now drink." Just then a bird sang.

"He doesn't pay attention," Nonna Graziella said. "That's the trouble."
And Nonna Graziella was right.

Every year little Anthony grew taller. Soon he was big enough to help on the farm.

"Here's a basket, Anthony. Go to the garden and pick the lettuce the way I showed you. Then bring it to me in the kitchen," Mama told him.
"*Sì*, Mama," Anthony said. And Anthony did.

"Oh, Anthony!" Mama said.

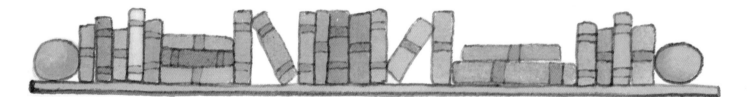

Now Anthony was old enough to go to school. Anthony loved school, but the teacher kept on saying, "*Attenzione*, Anthony—*per favore*—please pay attention!"

Because Anthony was the tallest boy in the class, the teacher asked him to stay after school one day and help tidy up the schoolroom.

"Anthony, would you please put all these books up on that shelf? We'll put the other things away when I come back. Are you paying attention to me, Anthony?"

"Ah, *sì, professore*. Up on the shelf." So Anthony did.

As Anthony grew older, and taller, he was needed on the farm.

"Anthony," Nonna Graziella said. "Take the lunches down to the field where the men are haying. And," Nonna Graziella added, "be sure to find a shady spot to put them so they don't get hot in the sun."

"*Sì*, Nonna," Anthony said.

Anthony looked around. There were no trees in the field. "I know," he said to himself. "I'll put the lunches under that haystack. They'll stay nice and cool there, and I'll just take a nap until it's time to eat."

So Anthony did.

"Anthony," Nonno Emilio called. "Wake up. Where is the food? We're hungry."

Anthony smiled a big smile. "I did just what Nonna Graziella said. I put the lunches where they would stay nice and cool. I put them under a haystack. I'll go get them right away."

Now Anthony was the tallest one in his whole family.
"It's from my side," Nonno Emilio said.
Everyone began to call him "Big Anthony."

"Big Anthony," Mama said one day, "go find your papa. The pasta is ready."

"*Sì*, Mama," Big Anthony said, and rushed out.

"And, Anthony, don't leave any of the gates open. Did you hear me?"

"*Sì*, Mama," Big Anthony shouted, "gates open!"

And Big Anthony did.

He left every single gate open.

"That's it," Papa said. "It's time for Big Anthony to go out into the world and earn his fortune."

"Before he ruins ours," Nonna Graziella said.

"*Arrivederci*, Big Anthony, *buona fortuna*—good luck," the family called as Big Anthony set out on his journey.

Down the highways and byways, Big Anthony strode south, whistling a happy tune. The whole world was ahead of him. How excited he was.

He walked and walked until the sun set. He arrived at a town called Pisa.

It was too dark to go any farther, so Big Anthony found a wall to sit against. He opened his sack and ate his supper. Before he knew it, he was fast asleep.

The birds woke him at dawn. He stood up, stretched, and opened his eyes. What he saw shocked him.

"I must have leaned too hard against the wall," he said to himself. "But I can fix it." And he rushed away before anyone was awake.

Off he went, down the road, pleased that he had fixed the tower.

Soon he came to a place called Firenze. Firenze was filled with art.

So Big Anthony got a job with an artist.

"Now, Anthony, the first thing I want you to do is to make the paints. See these colored powders? Mix each one with water and put them in jars. Do you understand?"

"*Sì, Maestro*," Big Anthony said.

"Let's see," Big Anthony said to himself after the artist had left the room, "I have to mix all these colors with the water and put them in jars."

So Big Anthony did.

"You've ruined my paints!" the artist shouted. "You're fired."
So Big Anthony traveled on until he reached Roma. Big Anthony
had never seen such beautiful buildings and so many churches.

Soon he came to a toll bridge that crossed the river that ran through the middle of the city.

"Two coins, please," the man at the bridge told him.

"I have no money," Big Anthony said. "But I'm here to get a job. If you let me cross, I promise to come back and pay you."

"Well, you're in luck. I need a helper. Would you like the job?" the man asked.

"*Sì, Signore,*" answered Big Anthony, looking around.

"You must collect a toll of two coins," the man said. "But not from the Cardinal. Are you paying attention?"

"Oh, *sì, Signore*," Big Anthony said. "From the Cardinal."

All day Big Anthony let everyone go across the bridge—for free.

Then up to the bridge came a long line of altar boys and priests, followed by the Cardinal.

Big Anthony let everyone cross without paying. But when the
Cardinal came up, Big Anthony shouted, "Halt. Two coins to cross."
"But *I* am the Cardinal."

"Sorry, *Cardinale,* but you must pay! Everyone else can cross for free,
but *you* must pay. My boss said so."

So Big Anthony left Roma and headed south until he arrived at
Napoli.

Luck was with him. No sooner had he walked into the city than
Big Anthony got a job as a waiter.

"Be sure to pay attention to the orders so you give the right food
to the right customer," the owner of the restaurant told him.

But Big Anthony didn't pay attention.

"I didn't order the eels. I hate eels."
"Where is my pizza?"
"Waiter, waiter, you gave me *zuppa*—soup. I ordered pasta!"

"Out! Out!" the owner shouted.

Just as Big Anthony left the restaurant, Mount Vesuvius, the volcano, erupted.

"Well," Big Anthony said, "at least *that's* not my fault."

Big Anthony headed south again until he came to the part of the country called Calabria.

He walked down a hill and came to a little village. There in the town square was a sign. Someone needed a helper, someone who lived in a little house up the hill.

Big Anthony climbed the hill to the little house and knocked on the door.

The rest is history.